For everyone who's ever felt misjudged or misunderstood.

Copyright © 2001 by William Kotzwinkle and Glenn Murray. Illustrations © 2001 by Audrey Colman.

Published by Frog, Ltd.

Frog, Ltd. books are distributed by North Atlantic Books, P.O. Box 12327, Berkeley, California 94712

ISBN-10: 1-58394-053-7 / ISBN-13: 978-1583-94053-2
Library of Congress Catalog Card Number 2001033450

Book design by Audrey Colman and Paula Morrison

Printed in Singapore

19 20 21 22 23 24 25 TWP 12 11 10 09 08 07

William Kotzwinkle and Glenn Murray
Walter the Farting Dog

illustrated by Audrey Colman

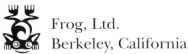

Frog, Ltd.
Berkeley, California

Betty and Billy brought Walter home from the dog pound. "Nobody wanted him," said Billy.

"But we love him," said Betty.

"Well, he smells awful," said their mother. "I think you'd better give him a bath."

Mother walked in and said, "He still smells awful."

And that's when they got the first clue. The tell-tale bubbles in the water.

"He's probably just a little nervous," said Mother, hopefully. "His stomach must be upset."

But Walter's stomach wasn't upset. Walter's stomach was fine. He felt perfectly normal. He just farted a lot.

He did it when he bathed. He did it when he played with Betty and Billy. He did it when he walked around the house.

He did it in the dining room. He did it in the kitchen. And he did it in his sleep.

"That dog farts morning, noon, and night," said Father.

"He can't help it, Daddy," said Betty and Billy.

They didn't mind Walter's farts.

"So what if he farts," Billy said to Betty when they were alone in their room with Walter.

Betty agreed. Walter agreed too. He sat there, looking innocently around, farting.

"Take him to the vet," said Father.

"Farting," said the vet, "or rectal flatulence, as we say in the medical profession," and prescribed a change in diet.

They gave Walter every kind of dog food. He farted. They tried him on cat food. They gave him hot dogs, hamburgers, and lettuce and tomato sandwiches.

They gave him fried chicken. They gave him
rabbit food. They made him a vegetarian.

"No matter what that dog eats, he turns it into
farts," roared Father.

Walter got the blame for everybody else's farts too. If Uncle Irv let one slip, he just went and stood near Walter.

Then all he had to say was, "Walter!"

And everyone would look at poor Walter.

"He has to go back to the pound," said Father.
  "No, Daddy, please," begged Betty and Billy.
"Don't send Walter away."
  "He goes tomorrow," said Father.
They pleaded. Walter farted.

It was all over. That night, Betty and Billy cried in their beds, and Walter looked at them unhappily.
  "Oh Walter," said Betty, "you've got to stop farting."
  "Because Father is going to send you back to the pound tomorrow," said Billy.

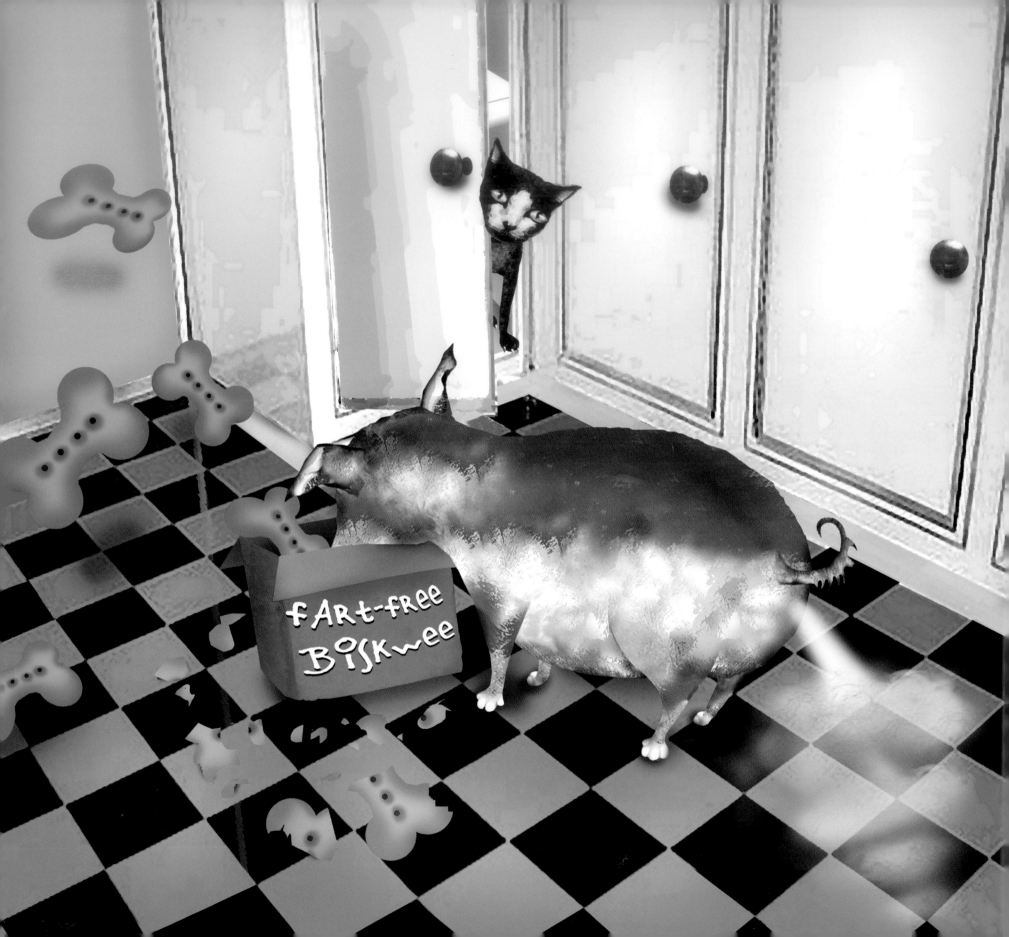

Walter knew how serious the situation was. He'd never see Betty and Billy again. He resolved to hold in his farts forever. When Betty and Billy fell asleep, he walked down to the kitchen to see if there was anything around to eat. He managed to open the cupboard door with his nose and found the 25-pound bag of low-fart dog biscuits the vet had prescribed for him, which had made him fart more. Even though he knew they made him fart more, he couldn't resist. He ate the entire bag. "Very tasty," said Walter to himself.

And then he went and lay down on the sofa.
A gigantic gas bubble began to build inside him.
"This is going to be trouble," he said to himself,
nervously. He was afraid of what might happen if
he let it go. He thought maybe the house would
explode. So he kept it in. It wasn't easy. In fact,
it was torture. But he had resolved never to fart
again. His future depended on it. As he lay there,
with his tail wrapped tightly between his legs, he
heard a noise at the window.

He watched it slowly open.

A pair of burglars came through.

They dropped silently into the kitchen.

"Watch out for the dog," said one of the burglars.

"He won't bite," said the other. "He's a wimp."
Walter might have bitten them, except he was so
filled with gas he couldn't move. They tied a rag
around his snout so he couldn't bark.

"Okay," whispered the first burglar, "let's clear
the place out."

They took everything they could get their hands
on. Walter wanted to stop them but he was having
unbearable gas pains. He rolled on his back, and
waved his paws in the air. He gnashed his teeth.

"We've got it all," said the second burglar.

"Let's go."

That's when Walter let it fly. It was the worst fart of his life. It made a tremendous noise and shot him across the room. A hideous cloud filled the air. The burglars clutched their throats, unable to breathe.

With tears in their eyes, they raced for the window. They tried to grab their bag with all the valuables in it, but their arms were too weak. "Let's...get...out...of...here..."

They jumped out the window and ran up the block, choking and gasping for air. Still blinded by Walter's attack, they stepped into the headlights of an approaching police car.

"Hold it right there!" said the policeman.

When Father and Mother came down in the morning, they found the open window. And they saw the bag with their valuables in it. And Walter was sitting beside it. He still had the rag tied around his snout. You'd have to say he looked heroic.

"He saved the silverware!" cried Mother.

"He saved the VCR!" cried Father. "Good dog, Walter! You're our dog, even if you do fart all the time."

And so the family learned to live with Walter,
the hero dog.

And that's the end of our tail.